Dear Pig Fans,

Pigs At Odds: Fun With Math and Games is the seve[nth] in the Pigs Will Be Pigs math series. It's all about PRO[BABILITY] or the chance of something happening. When I was i[n] school, that word frightened me, as did just about every[thing] that had to do with math. I never realized that math was all around us in our daily lives. That's why I wrote the Pigs Will Be Pigs books, which (by the way) are all based on true family adventures. My family loves to go to the county fair every summer. We always play games and try to win prizes. Sometimes we get lucky. One time I had a great idea—having the Pigs take chances on games would be a fun way to learn about probability. So follow these easy steps:

1) Read **Pigs At Odds** just for fun!

2) Go back and read the story again. Look at all the instructions for the games. Decide if these games are fair. Can you win on luck alone, or do you need special skills?

3) Mr. Pig tosses a penny to decide if they will go on rides first or play games first. Practice the odds. Toss a penny one hundred times. How many times did it come out heads? How many times tails?

4) Answer the math questions at the end of the book. You can do this by yourself, with your parents, or with your teacher.

Remember the Pig Family Motto:

MATH + READING = FUN

Love,

Amy Axelrod

P.S. For Parents and Teachers Only

The Pigs Will Be Pigs books have been designed around the National Council of Teachers of Mathematics's Thirteen Standards. Use them as picture book read-alouds initially, and then as vehicles to introduce, reinforce, and review the concepts and skills particular to each title.

Pigs at Odds

Fun with Math and Games

story by **Amy Axelrod**

pictures by **Sharon McGinley-Nally**

Aladdin Paperbacks

New York   London   Toronto   Sydney   Singapore

Mr. Pig and the piglets were raring to go.

"We want to go on the rides," said the piglets.

"And I want to try my luck at the games," said Mr. Pig.

"Hold your horses," said Mrs. Pig. "Both are great ideas, except for one thing."

"What's that?" asked the piglets.

"We can't be in two places at the same time," she said.

"No problem," said Mr. Pig. "Why don't I just flip a coin? Heads we play games first, and tails we go on rides first."

"Fair enough," said Mrs. Pig, and she handed Mr. Pig a penny.

"All right!" said the piglets.

LET'S

ROCK AND ROLL!

The Pigs tumbled down slides, steered bumper cars, and dipped up and down on the carousel.

"Kids," asked Mr. Pig, "are you ready to go win some prizes now?"
"Not yet," they said. "We want to go on
the Colossal Coaster."

"But you're not tall enough," said Mrs. Pig.
The piglets grinned and pointed to the sign.

The Pigs wobbled over to the games.

"C'mon, dear," said Mrs. Pig. "Let's take a chance on the spin of the wheel."

Mr. and Mrs. Pig each put down one quarter at four different times, but the wheel never landed on the right space.

The piglets grew tired of waiting and got tattooed at the booth next door.

"Dad, try the basketball game," said the piglets. "They've got good prizes."

Mr. Pig bounced the basketball into the basket on the first try.

"Lucky shot," said the piglets. "Do it again!"

But after Mr. Pig tried for the eighth time, Mrs. Pig tapped him on the shoulder and said, "Dear, I don't think the odds are in your favor."

"Just one more time," said Mr. Pig as he put down another two dollars. "I know I've got a good chance of winning."

"I think we've got a better chance of seeing a two-headed snake," said Mrs. Pig.

See the Amazing Snake Charmer

Mrs. Pig and the piglets dragged Mr. Pig down the midway.

"You were right, dear," said Mr. Pig. "I should have quit while I was ahead of the game."

The piglets shared a bucket of rings while Mr. Pig tested his strength.

"Sweetie, why don't you try bowling?" suggested Mrs. Pig.

"No, you go ahead. That's more up your alley," said Mr. Pig.

So Mrs. Pig gave it a try. She walked away with two medium-size toys for the piglets.

"I'm down to my bottom dollar," said Mr. Pig.

"Well then," said Mrs. Pig, "here's the perfect game for you and the children—three tries for a dollar. I have a hunch you're going to win this time."

Mr. Pig came in first and surprised Mrs. Pig by giving her his free game.

"Don't you want to try for a giant prize?" she asked him.

"I have all the prizes I need," said Mr. Pig, giving her a hug. "Besides, the fun is really in the trying."

"Your mom won, so go right ahead, kids," said the barker.
"Pick the prize of your choice."

The piglets grinned and pointed to the sign.

Mr. and Mrs. Pig gripped the bar tightly and screamed, "We should have quit when we were ahead of the . . . "

Probability is the chance that something will happen. The probability or chance of the sun rising in the morning is 100 percent because it always happens. The probability of the moon turning bright pink is 0 percent because it never happens. The probability of you getting a letter in the mail can be anywhere from 0 percent to 100 percent, depending on how many friends you have who write to you!

What Makes a Game Fair?

If every player has equal odds, or chances, of winning, then the game is fair.

Mr. Pig needed the spinner to land on September to win. What is the probability that this will happen? Mrs. Pig needed the spinner to land on November. What is the probability that this will happen? Mr. and Mrs. Pig played this game four times. Did their odds of winning change with each game? Is the game fair?

Ten players can sit at the Fill the Water Balloon Game at one time. What are the odds of winning? Can you show it as a fraction?

Bonus: How much money did the Pigs spend on rides and games?

First Aladdin Paperbacks edition July 2003
Text copyright © 2000 by Amy Axelrod
Illustrations copyright © 2000 by Sharon McGinley-Nally

ALADDIN PAPERBACKS
An imprint of Simon & Schuster
Children's Publishing Division
1230 Avenue of the Americas
New York, NY 10020

Also available in a Simon & Schuster Books for Young Readers hardcover edition.
Designed by Anahid Hamparian
The text of this book was set in 17point Baskerville.
The illustrations are rendered in ink, watercolor, and acrylic.

Manufactured in China
2 4 6 8 10 9 7 5 3 1

The Library of Congress has cataloged the hardcover edition as follows:

Pigs at odds : fun with math and games / story by Amy Axelrod ; pictures by Sharon McGinley-Nally. —1st ed.
p.   cm.
Summary: While trying their luck at various games at the county fair, members
of the Pig family find out what the odds are that they will go home as winners.
Includes an explanation of odds and probability.
ISBN 0-689-81566-2
[1. Fairs—Fiction. 2. Games—Fiction. 3. Probabilities—Fiction. 4. Pigs—Fiction.]
I. McGinley-Nally, Sharon, ill. II. Title.
PZ7.A96155Pi 2000
[Fic]—dc21
99-14518
CIP
ISBN 0-689-86144-3 (Aladdin pbk.)

For my niece,
Elana Beth Snyder
—A. A.

To Emma Leigh Conklin
and Graeham Conklin
—S. M-N.